This book belongs to

Malia Richards

from Aunt Merline

Christmas 2015

Copyright © 2014

make believe ideas ltd

The Wilderness, Berkhamsted, Hertfordshire, HP4 2AZ, UK.
501 Nelson Place, P.O. Box 141000, Nashville, TN 37214-1000, USA.

www.makebelieveideas.com

Written by Tim Bugbird.
Illustrated by Lara Ede.
Designed by Ellie Fahy.

Georgie
the Gingerbread Fairy

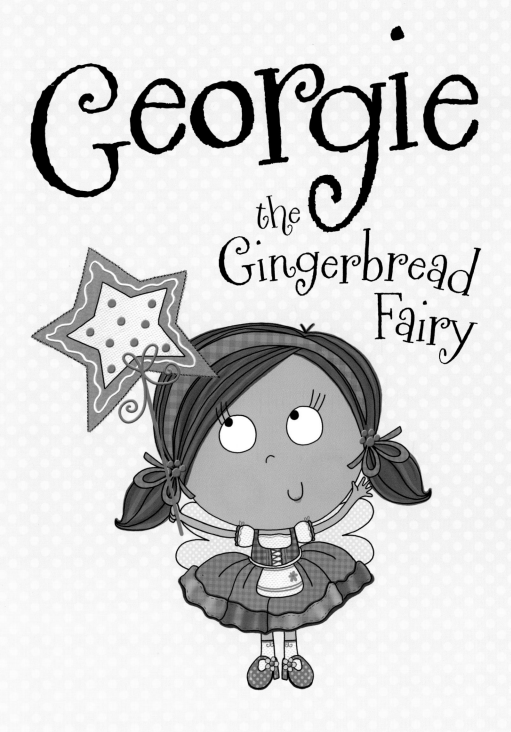

Tim Bugbird • Lara Ede

make
believe
ideas

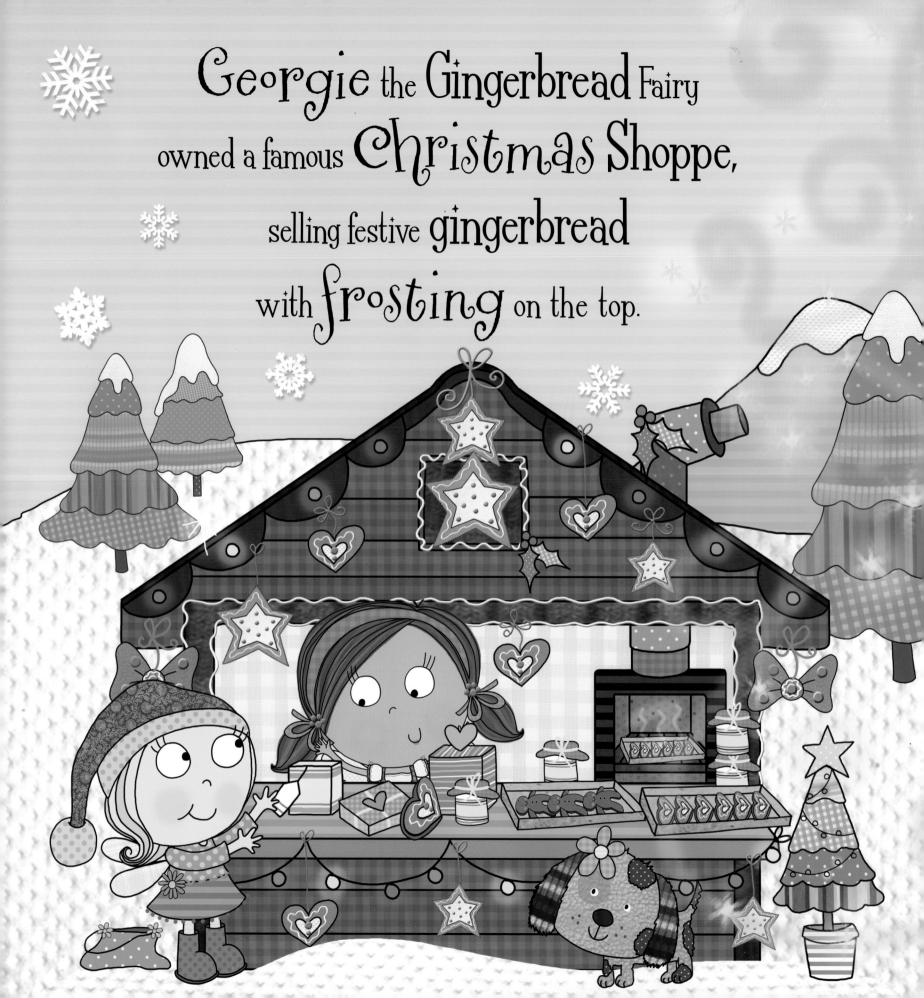

Georgie the Gingerbread Fairy owned a famous Christmas Shoppe, selling festive gingerbread with frosting on the top.

Every year, sweet, swirling puffs
would scent the winter air —
the smell of baking gingerbread,
made with loving care!

Then one day when baking
with her best friends, Jo and Sue,

It was Teena the Tinsel Fairy!
She was building a brand-new store,
with golden walls, a star-shaped hatch
and glitter roof to floor!

"Call me Tee," the fairy said.
"I've just flown in — I'm new!
Come inside, why don't you?
I'll show you what I do!"

"Wow!" said Georgie. "Woo!" said Jo.
(And Sue couldn't make a sound.)
They stepped inside, with hard hats on,
and slowly looked around.

Teena's Tinsellator was right before their eyes,
making **glittering** garlands and **gifts** in every size!

Soon Teena's store was open,
and the fairies flocked to buy
her SPARKLY, plastic treasures —
they really caught your eye!

But no one came to Georgie's Shoppe –
her goods were so last year.
Gingerbread was out of style –
that soon became quite clear!

So Georgie tried her very best
to make her Shoppe more inviting,

Georgie's
Gingerbread

but next to glitter, gingerbread
just did not look exciting.

Teena's Treasures

Turning off her **oven** and **locking** her Shoppe door,

Georgie thought, "They don't need me or my **gingerbread** anymore."

As Christmas Day got closer,
Teena did a booming trade.
The fairies loved her treasures
and the sparkling homes they made.

Fairy Land was **beautiful**;
it all looked so **fantastic**.

But something **strange** now filled the air . . .

the smell of shiny plastic!

The **fairies** held their noses —
it really wasn't **pleasant**.
The **Tinsellator** was puffing out
an **unappealing** present!

The smelly smog made Georgie think,

"If we found a way to sell

the scent of baking gingerbread,

the Shoppe would soon do well!"

"I think I **gave up** far too soon. I really can't turn down this chance to let **tradition** save **Christmas** in our town!"

Jo and Sue went straight to work.
Georgie waved her wand into action.
Together, they built a brilliant thing:
an amazing, smell-catching contraption!

They bottled the smell of gingerbread
and labeled it "Fairy Delight."

"It'll be a best seller!" Georgie cried,
crossing her fingers tight.

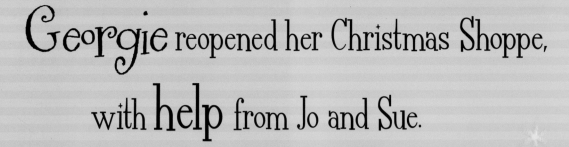

Georgie reopened her Christmas Shoppe,
with **help** from Jo and Sue.

Fairy Delight flew off the shelves
and gingerbread sold again, too!

Georgie was back in business –
having Teena next door would be fine.

Now Christmas was perfectly sparkly
and the air smelled simply divine!

Together, the FAIRIES discovered that when old and new combine,

it makes the season perfect and a truly SPECIAL time.